THE CASE OF THE
HORRIBLE
SWAMP MONSTER

THE CASE OF THE

HORRIBLE

SWAMP MONSTER

Drew Stevenson

ILLUSTRATED BY

Susan Swan

DODD, MEAD & COMPANY
New York

Wolfman howls at the moon so full,
Dracula lurks with fangs so cruel,
Godzilla, Mothra, and Rodan
Each have a turn at eating Japan.

The Mummy walks and feels no pity,
King Kong tramples New York City,
Frankenstein is sure to come along soon
And maybe the Creature from the Black Lagoon.

Monsters mean and monsters mad,
Monsters happy and monsters sad,
Monsters small and monsters tall,
Monsters, monsters, we love you all.
                    —*J. Huntley English, M.H.*

"One, two, three, four, five, six. One, two, three, four, five, six. One, two, three, four, five, six . . . "

I sat at my desk and held my breath as Mrs. Phillips quickly counted the rest of the class.

"All right, boys and girls," she said when she finished. "All Number One's gather over here, all Number Two's over there."

I didn't hear any more. My name is Raymond Almond and I sit in the first desk in the first row. I'm a Number One. This number business was Mrs. Phillips' idea. She's really into it. For our sixth-grade spring project, we are supposed to work in teams of six. Mrs. Phillips said that the fairest way to divide into teams was to count off. Actually I wouldn't have worried about who was in my group except that there was one person in class I *didn't* want to be teamed with.

"Just my crummy luck to get stuck with you in *my* group," Verna Wilkes hissed at me as we arrived in

the same corner of the room at the same time.

I groaned. Talk about crummy luck! One chance out of six, and I end up in the same group with Verna Wilkes, the bossiest, most stuck-up kid in the whole school.

"Who says it's *your* group?" I muttered.

"You know darned well I'll be team leader," Verna said in her snootiest voice. "Some people, like me, are natural leaders. Others, like you, are born to follow. Like a horse's rear end."

Before I could come back with an appropriate insult, Mrs. Phillips told us to form our desks into group circles and talk about what we'd like to do for our projects.

I looked at group Number One. Besides Verna and myself, there were Geoffrey Powell, Annie Shaw, Bill Chambers, and Angela Rossini.

"All right," Verna said, immediately taking control of things. "Anybody got any ideas about what our project can be?"

Geoffrey Powell started to say something but Verna cut him off.

"I have a great idea," she announced. "As you know, I got a movie camera for Christmas."

I groaned again. Since Verna got that stupid movie camera, she hasn't let anyone forget it. She even brought it to class, not once but four times. Verna gave me one of her famous if-we-weren't-in-class-I'd-wring-your-neck looks and kept on talking.

"Let's make our own movie," she said excitedly, "with a real story and everything!"

"Hey, that's a good idea," Geoffrey said, lighting up. "I can write the script."

"And I'll be director and cameraperson," Verna added.

"What kind of movie will be make?" Angela asked.

"A monster movie!" Verna answered. "Angela, you and Bill will play a husband and wife who are terrorized by a monster. You'll make a lovely couple."

Both Bill and Angela blushed and shrugged their shoulders modestly.

"And Annie," Verna went on, "you can be in charge of costuming."

Now everyone in the group was enthusiastically applauding Verna's idea. Everybody but me, that is.

"Hey, wait a minute," I finally piped up. "What part will I play?"

You'd think I'd have learned about keeping my mouth shut where Verna Wilkes was concerned.

"You, Raymond?" she said in a sicky-sweet voice.

"With your looks, you could only play the part of the horrible monster."

The whole group exploded with laughter while I sat there feeling like a lobster in a hot pot.

"Where are we going to shoot this monster movie?" Annie Shaw asked. "It should be someplace scary."

"How about that, Miss Alfred Hitchcock?" I said smugly. "Where are you going to find a scary enough place here in little old Barkley, Pennsylvania?"

Verna stood up and made her voice as dramatic as possible.

"How about Lost Swamp?"

Everyone inhaled so loudly it sounded like a balloon factory.

"Lost Swamp?" Bill Chambers finally said in a quivery voice. "They say weird things happen there."

Verna suddenly leaned forward and pounded the desk with her fist. "Wilkes is my name! Movie-making is my game! Lost Swamp it is!"

I looked around at the other scared faces. We all were afraid of Lost Swamp, but we were even more afraid of Verna Wilkes.

2

Two weeks later it was Saturday and I was running up the long sidewalk to Verna's house. We were supposed to meet there before heading out to the swamp to shoot the movie. I was late, as usual.

Verna and her parents live in a big house in Barkley's classiest neighborhood. Mrs. Wilkes is president of the only bank in town. Verna's father is a professional sports photographer. He has to be away a lot, which may be why he showers Verna with expensive gifts like movie cameras.

I rang the doorbell and Mrs. Wilkes answered. She was wearing a tweed suit and smelled like fancy soap. Mrs. Wilkes is an attractive woman. She sort of looks like an older version of Verna, although I hate admitting that Verna is kinda cute with her red hair and green eyes.

"Come in, Raymond," Mrs. Wilkes said. "The other kids are up in Verna's room."

I knew right where to go. Mrs. Wilkes and my mother are good friends. Whenever they get together, Verna and I usually get stuck with each other.

As I headed for the stairs I remembered my manners. I was about to ask how she was when I noticed she was staring off into space with a worried look on her face. That wasn't like her. She's usually a very up kind of person. I kept on going.

The door to Verna's room was closed. I guess I should have knocked first. As I opened the door it banged into Verna, who was standing in front of it.

Angela, Bill, Annie, and Geoffrey were sitting on the floor munching on potato chips and dip.

"You're late," Verna said icily as she rubbed her back where the door had hit her.

"Sorry," I mumbled, trying to take my place on the floor without any more fuss. But I accidentally kicked over the bowl of chips. Then I sat in them with a loud, crunching sound.

No sooner had I gotten settled than Verna waved her hand in the air.

"All right, cast and crew," she exclaimed. "Let's roll."

"But I didn't get any chips," I protested as I stood up.

Verna leaned so close to me I could see chives from the dip on her molars.

"It looks like all of the chips are on the seat of your pants," she hissed.

"Verna!" an angry voice said from the door.

12

We turned and saw Mrs. Wilkes standing there with her hands on her hips and a furious look on her face.

"I thought I told you to clean up this room!" she said angrily. "We'll talk about this later, young lady."

I looked at Mrs. Wilkes in surprise as she stomped away. Unlike my mother, Mrs. Wilkes isn't the yelling type. I hadn't seen her this mad since last summer when Verna pushed me in the goldfish pond in the backyard.

"What's the matter with your mother?" I asked.

Verna shrugged her shoulders. "I'm not sure. She won't talk about it. I think maybe she had a fight with Dad."

We quickly left the house before Verna could get into any more trouble. We stopped by the garage to pick up the monster costume Annie had made for me. It was covered with a sheet so I couldn't see what it looked like.

As we walked along, the houses gradually gave way to countryside. Half a mile beyond the town limits, we turned right on an old dirt road that wound its way down through a thickly wooded valley. The bottom of the valley opened up on a thin stretch of grassland bordering a wide pool of water. Beyond the pool lay the dreaded swamp.

Before I go any further in my story, I'd better explain why we all acted like mice at a cat banquet when

Verna mentioned Lost Swamp. The name alone should tip you off. It got its name from all kinds of stories about people getting lost in it and never being seen again.

I once asked my dad about it. He just laughed and said that those old stories had been around since he was a kid. As far as he knew, no one had ever gotten lost in the swamp, let alone disappeared in it. His words didn't do much to put my mind at ease. Dad's an incurable optimist. He always sees the sunny side of every catastrophe. Like father, like son, we're not!

Everyone had been chattering away as we walked along, but, as we approached the pool, the silence got as thick as yesterday's chowder. I had only been to the swamp once in my life. A couple of years ago Bill Chambers had bet me I wouldn't stay in the swamp by myself for an hour. I lost the bet.

My heart sank as I looked at the vast bog that stretched out before us. It was just as scary as I remembered. I felt as if I were ice skating in my swim trunks. I mean, I was cold all over.

There it was. Lost Swamp. A mass of twisted, ugly trees, choking vines, mushy ground, and black pools. The air was musty and damp smelling. Back in town the late spring day had been sunny and warm. Down here it seemed darker and chillier.

Verna was pulling stuff out of the shopping bag she had brought along. First she put on sunglasses and a beret. A tiny megaphone came next. She looked like a director in one of those old-time movies.

"All right, everyone!" she hollered into the megaphone. "Quiet on the set!"

It was a dumb thing to say, since everyone already was quiet as death.

"Annie, get the monster costume ready."

While Annie uncovered the costume, Verna bustled around surveying the area. I have to admit she made the place seem less scary. It would take a lot more than a treacherous swamp to frighten Verna Wilkes!

"A perfect location for a monster movie," Verna proclaimed, practically patting herself on the back. "What atmosphere!"

When I saw my costume I couldn't believe my eyes. It was made out of cardboard and was tall and narrow, with a pointed top. Annie had drawn a huge mouth on the front, with fangs dripping blood. The whole thing was painted a bright orange. It looked like a giant, man-eating carrot. I mean, it had been scarier with the sheet over it.

Bill and Angela were spreading a blanket on the ground and pulling sandwiches out of the picnic basket they had brought.

"I don't suppose there are any potato chips in there?" I asked, walking over.

"Forget the chips!" Verna screamed through her megaphone right in my ear, almost making my hair stand up. "All right, Bill and Angela. Our opening shot will be the two of you having a nice romantic picnic by the water's edge."

"Who would be dumb enough to come to a swamp for a romantic picnic?" I said softly so Verna wouldn't hear and come after me with her megaphone. Annie heard me and giggled.

Verna was aiming her camera now. "Lights, camera, action!"

For the next couple of minutes she filmed Bill and Angela sitting on the blanket having their picnic. Whenever they talked they would wave their arms to make it look as if a real conversation was going on.

While Verna was busy filming, I took the opportunity to pick her megaphone up off the ground and hide it behind a bush.

"Cut!" she finally hollered. "O.K., Raymond, into the monster costume." She retrieved the megaphone.

Down by the pool, Annie helped me slip the costume over my head. Since I'm tall and skinny, it fit perfectly. At least no one will recognize me in here, I thought gratefully. It was then that I noticed there were no holes for me to see out of.

"Don't worry," Annie reassured me. "You aren't going far."

"According to Geoffrey's script," Verna directed us, "the monster has just come out of the slimy swamp. The couple is terrified. Bill, you run over and grab a club and begin to fight the creature."

"A club?" I squeaked from somewhere inside the carrot.

"Hey, wait a minute!" Angela protested. "I'm not going to just sit around acting scared and let a man fight my battles for me."

"You're right, Angela," Verna agreed. "You grab a club, too."

"Two clubs?" I groaned.

"Raymond," Verna said. "You just move around looking scary. Ready? Lights, camera, action!"

18

With a horrible roar, or at least as horrible a roar as I could come out with, I moved forward to terrorize the poor couple. I got almost ten feet before Bill and Angela began to defend themselves. *Wham*! One of them hit me with a club and almost knocked me over.

"Hey! Take it easy!" I yelled.

Wham! The other one took a crack at the monster.

"I said watch it!" I hollered.

Wham! *Wham*!

Now I could hear Verna yelling at me. "Raymond! Raymond! You're going the wrong way! Attack! Attack! Attack!"

"When you're getting beaten to death, you retreat, retreat, retreat!" I screamed as I moved quickly away from the blows.

In my haste to get away from the defenseless humans I had forgotten one thing. The pool! Too late! The next thing I knew I had run off the bank and fallen face flat into the cold slimy water.

The last thing I heard before I got an earful of algae was Verna hollering, "Perfect, Raymond! That's perfect!"

What with the water and my thrashing around, the costume quickly disintegrated. I came to the surface gasping for air and began swimming frantically toward the bank. Soon the water was shallow enough for wading, but I only managed to get two steps before my feet stuck.

"Quicksand! Quicksand!" I screamed. "Help me!"

But no one helped me. They were too busy rolling around on the ground laughing. And who could blame them? After all, the mud was only up to my ankles and I was standing there looking like Moby Duck. Worst of all, Verna was still filming.

"I've got a great idea," Geoffrey hooted. "Let's keep the movie as it is. Instead of a scary movie, it'll be a comedy."

I groaned and wished that I really was sinking in quicksand.

4

My mom called me to the phone the next afternoon. It was Verna on the line.

"Raymond?" she said. "Come over right away."

"Why?" I asked coldly. I was still pretty miffed about Saturday's fiasco.

"Dad's off in Florida taking pictures of the Pirates' spring training camp but I got his assistant to develop the film for me."

"No, thank you," I replied in a voice that could have frozen the entire state of Florida.

"But you *have* to see the movie," Verna persisted. "There's something weird about it."

"Yeah. Me!" I said angrily.

"Besides you. Please come over."

It's not often Verna says please when she's not talking to an adult. I felt myself giving in. Maybe I could convince her to can the movie and shoot another one. Besides, I was just a little bit curious to see myself on the silver screen.

"Oh, all right," I said, trying to sound as if I were doing her a big favor. "I'll come over."

A few minutes later I was sitting in the huge playroom of the Wilkes house watching Verna thread her projector. It was another gift from her father.

Pretty soon the film was rolling on the screen. I scrunched down in my seat. Already I could feel my ears getting red. There were Bill and Angela having their picnic, waving their arms as they talked. Rather than having a conversation, they seemed to be swatting mosquitoes. Then the not-so-horrible swamp monster appeared, looking like a vegetable in search of a salad. Next the poor monster was being beaten to death. Splash! The monster fell into the pool. And then there was Raymond Almond looking like his namesake. A nut!

"Listen, Verna," I said when the movie was over. "If you show this to anyone, I'll report you to the S.P.C.M."

"What's the S.P.C.M.?" she asked.

"The Society for the Prevention of Cruelty to Monsters."

"Did you see anything strange?" Verna asked, ignoring my sarcasm.

"Just the dumbest movie ever," I answered sullenly.

"That's all I thought the first time I saw it," Verna said. "Now I want you to watch it again."

"Do I have to?"

"Only this time," Verna went on, "don't watch

yourself making a fool of yourself. Watch the background closely.''

I watched the movie again. This time around I did
as she said. At first, I didn't see anything strange. Not
until the part where I fell in the water, that is. Suddenly my eye caught something in the background.
Something very strange. Something I couldn't explain. I felt my heart beating a little faster.

"Play it again, Sam," I said when it was over.

This time as I watched, I leaned forward in my seat.
Then I saw it again! Now my heart was racing as if I
had just run the two minute mile. There I was on the
screen helplessly trying to climb out of the water. And
there, in the background on the other side of the pool,
something else *was* climbing out of the water.

It looked something like a human being but it definitely wasn't human. It was a dark green color and it
was covered with slime. All you could see was its back
as it climbed out of the pool. Once on land, it hob-
bled awkwardly into the swamp and quickly disappeared. It was only on the screen for a couple of seconds all together.

"Why didn't we see it?" I asked when Verna turned
on the lights.

"Because you were in the water doing your famous
flounder imitation and the rest of us were watching
you," Verna answered.

24

"But what was it?" I whispered.

"You tell me," Verna said grimly.

I could feel a bead of sweat trickling down my back. My hands were cold and clammy.

"It looked like . . . it looked like. . ." I stammered.

"Spit it out, Raymond," Verna urged me.

"It looked like a real swamp monster!" I finally blurted.

"I agree," Verna said, and for the first time since I had known her, which is all my life, there was a look of fear on her face.

We sat in shocked silence for awhile.

"I hate to say this," Verna finally said, "but I think we'd better consult that weird friend of yours."

I nodded my head numbly in agreement. This definitely looked like a case for J. Huntley English, M.H.

5

Although we don't see each other a lot, Jonathan
Huntley English is one of my best friends. The reason
we don't see each other much is because Huntley goes
to a school for gifted students in Pittsburgh. If he went
to regular public school like me he would also be in
the sixth grade but he goes to this special school because he's super smart.

Huntley's house is about half a mile from Verna's.
I ran most of the way. Mrs. English answered the door.
She's a real nice lady. She works as a teller at Mrs.
Wilkes's bank.

"Why, Raymond!" she said, letting me in. "How
nice to see you. Huntley's upstairs in his office."

Mrs. English always makes a big fuss over me when
I come to visit. You see, Huntley doesn't have many
friends. Most kids around Barkley don't even know
he exists. Those that do think he's an oddball. Don't
feel sorry for him, though. He's a loner who likes it
that way.

I went upstairs. Since Huntley is an only child, Mr.
and Mrs. English let him use the third bedroom for

his office. As always, I paused to admire the sign on the door:

The M.H. stands for Monster Hunter. Huntley adds it to the end of his name the way doctors add M.D. or professors Ph.D. to theirs. Huntley is very serious about being an M.H. I have to give him credit for that, since people don't exactly wear out the carpet rushing to his office to consult him. I mean there just aren't a lot of monsters in Barkley, Pennsylvania.

Huntley was sitting at his desk reading the Pittsburgh *Post-Gazette* and listening to some weird music on his stereo. He's as short and chunky as I am tall and skinny, and he wears thick glasses that make him look very serious.

"Hello, Raymond!" he said, waving at me. "Come in! Come in!"

"How goes it, Hunt?" I asked as I sat down.

Huntley put the newspaper aside. "I was just reading that there was another Bigfoot sighting out in British Columbia. Maybe you and I should go there and investigate?"

That's the way Huntley talks. As if all I had to do was say yes and we would fly out to the Pacific Northwest to chase Bigfoot.

27

I shook my head. "It looks like we may have our own unexplained phenomena right here in Barkley to investigate."

Huntley leaned forward excitedly. "Tell me more, Raymond!"

"I don't think I can describe it," I said. "You'd better come over to Verna Wilkes's house and see for yourself."

Huntley sighed and sat back in his swivel chair. "I don't think so, Raymond."

"Why not?" I asked in amazement.

"The last time you took me to Verna's house she said I had bats in my belfry."

"Well, she won't say it this time," I promised. "It was Verna who asked me to come get you."

He still looked unconvinced. While he thought about it, I glanced around the room. Huntley's bookshelves are filled with almost every kind of monster, science fiction, and ghost book imaginable. The walls are covered with horror movie posters. A bust of Count Dracula sits on his desk. There's even a dinosaur mobile hanging from the ceiling.

Now it was my turn to lean forward. "I'm talking about a monster, Huntley. A monster right here in Barkley."

That got him! No one, not even Verna Wilkes, could scare J. Huntley English, M.H., away from a monster hunt.

28

"Lead on, Raymond!" he said, reaching for his sunglasses.

I paused at the door while he turned off the stereo.

"What was that weird music, anyway?" I asked.

"A new record I got. It's different theme songs from different monster movies. That last song was from the movie *Mothra Moves Against Moscow*."

I laughed. "It sounded more like 'Mothra Moults Over Maine.'"

Huntley wasn't amused. Like I said, he takes his monsters very seriously.

6

"So when's he gonna say something?" Verna hissed in my ear.

She was referring to Huntley, who had just finished viewing the movie for the sixth time and was now deep in thought.

"*Sssshhhh.* He's thinking," I whispered back. "And by the way, don't say anything about his having birds in the bathtub."

"That's bats in the belfry," Verna corrected me.

"Incredible!" Huntley suddenly exclaimed, jumping to his feet.

"So what's it all about, Hunt?" I asked.

Huntley was pacing back and forth rubbing his hands together.

"It's a monster all right," he replied. "Half man, half reptile. Imagine it being right here under our very noses!"

"Half man, half reptile?" I asked in amazement. "How did that happen?"

"That's easy," Verna snorted. "Some princess married a frog and that's their son out there."

I bit my lip to keep from laughing.

31

Huntley looked very solemn. "This is no joking matter. What we have here is the greatest scientific discovery in all of history."

"So what do we do?" I asked. "Show our movie to some science professors at the University of Pittsburgh?"

"Better than that, Raymond," Huntley answered. "We'll show them the creature itself."

My big mouth fell open. "But to do that we'll have to . . . we'll have to . . ." I couldn't finish.

Huntley finished it for me. "That's right, Raymond. We'll have to catch it."

Now Verna was picking up Huntley's enthusiasm. "Capture a swamp monster? Talk about a great class project!"

"Verna," Huntley said in a faraway voice. "We may be talking about a Nobel Prize."

"Say, what about the others?" I piped up. "Angela, Bill, Geoffrey, and Annie are in on this, too."

"The movie will still be their class project," Verna pointed out, "but we're not including them in our monster hunt. They're the hysterical types. What we need are cool heads."

I didn't want to admit to Verna that I was feeling rather hysterical about the whole crazy plan myself. I mean, three kids taking on a real living, breathing, moving monster? It sounded dangerous. It *was* dangerous!

"So what's our next move?" Verna asked our resident expert.

"We meet here just after dark," Huntley replied. "Raymond, you bring a long pole. Verna, you supply a flashlight. I'll bring the rest of the equipment we'll need."

His words shook me up so much I forgot to ask him why we needed a long pole.

"After dark?" I croaked. "You mean we're going to Lost Swamp at night?"

Huntley nodded his head. "We'll stand a better chance of sneaking up on the creature."

"And he'll stand a better chance of sneaking up on us," I said weakly.

Huntley put his hand on my shoulder. "Great scientific discoveries don't come easy, Raymond."

"I . . . I don't think my mom will let me leave the house after dark on a Sunday night," I said in a last ditch effort to get out of the expedition. "I mean, with school tomorrow and everything."

"Just tell her that you and I are still working on our class project," Verna suggested. "It's the truth."

"Don't worry, Raymond," Huntley added. "We won't stay out late. Maybe we'll even be lucky and get back real early."

"Yeah," I thought grimly to myself. "Or maybe we won't get back at all."

7

If the swamp was scary during the day, it was an absolute nightmare in the dark. We stood beside the big pool and gazed silently across the black water. The trees of the swamp were like monsters themselves. Their twisting branches looked like tentacles waiting to grab us. Who knew what horrible dangers were lurking in the secret depths of Lost Swamp?

I looked over at Huntley. He was wearing his monster-hunting outfit. On his back was a large knapsack. On his head he wore a jungle-style pith helmet. All three of us wore dark clothes and boots. We looked like a commando squad from some war movie.

We walked around the pool to where the narrow strip of grassland arched into the swamp. Soon we were standing at the spot where the monster had climbed out of the pool. Huntley took Verna's flashlight and shone it on the ground.

"Look!" he whispered excitedly.

I looked down and gasped. There in the mud was a huge webbed footprint!

"O.K., Raymond," Huntley whispered to me. "You lead the way into the swamp. Before you take a step, poke the ground with your pole."

"Why?" I asked.

"We don't want to step into any quicksand," was his answer.

I wasn't too thrilled with my role as poleperson but I figured I'd come this far so there was no turning back now. Taking a deep breath, I plunged into the bushes.

It was slow going, what with having to poke the pole in the ground with each step and the thick prickly branches and bushes snagging our clothes. Luckily we didn't hit any quicksand, just lots of watery ground.

About two hundred feet into the swamp, we came to a patch of fairly solid earth where Huntley drew us into a tight circle under a large tree.

"Here's where we'll set up an ambush for the monster," he whispered, looking around.

"Why don't we tie Raymond to a tree and use him as bait?" Verna suggested helpfully.

"I have our bait right here," Huntley said, reaching into his knapsack. He pulled out a plastic bowl. After removing the cover, he put the bowl on the ground.

"What is it?" I asked.

"Chili," he answered. "We had it for dinner to-night."

Verna chuckled. "Let's hope it's a Mexican monster," she said.

Huntley ignored her and reached into the big shopping bag he had been carrying. Out came a large net. Next he pulled a rope from the knapsack and handed it to me.

"Here's the plan," he whispered. "Verna and I will climb the tree with the net. Raymond, you hide in the bushes over there. When the monster comes to eat the chili, Verna and I will drop the net over him. Once he's good and tangled, Raymond will run over and tie him up."

It sure sounded like I was getting stuck with the most hazardous duty. As I stood on the ground and watched Verna trying to help a huffing and puffing Huntley up into the tree, I suddenly felt very alone. Here I was in a jungle about to do battle with a monster. Could I really be only a short walk from town where my father, mother, and little brother were right at this very minute?

After Verna and Huntley disappeared among the branches, I took my place in the bushes and settled down to wait. Everything was as dark as a licorice factory and deathly quiet. The only sound was an occasional gurgle of swamp gas in some nearby pool. I

36

tried not to think of deadly snakes slithering around my legs. How I envied them in the tree!

And then I heard it. Faintly at first but growing louder with each passing second. We weren't alone in the swamp! Something was definitely coming our way.

I held my breath and felt my heart jump with each approaching step. Beads of sweat broke out on my forehead, and I clutched the rope so tightly it burned my hands. South of my belt buckle, my knees were knocking.

And then it was in the clearing with us. I could only see its outline but I knew it was the monster. I suddenly realized how dumb Huntley's plan was. There was no way I was going to get near the beast with a rope or anything else.

As the monster lumbered closer and closer to the bushes where I was hiding, I felt my nerve breaking. When it was about ten feet from me, my courage snapped like a guitar string at a rock concert.

With a scream of terror, I bolted out of the bushes. I had every intention of running full blast until I was safely under my own bed at home. Unfortunately my path of retreat took me under the tree where Huntley and Verna were waiting. Down came the net over my head. I fell flat on my face in a hopelessly tangled mess.

As I struggled desperately to free myself, I watched

in horror as the creature moved toward me. He was just about on top of me when Verna did the bravest thing I'd ever seen.

With a battle cry that was a cross between a Tarzan yell and an elephant with a stomachache, Verna leaped from her limb onto the monster's back.

Now it was the monster's turn to howl as it ran around the clearing with Verna clinging tightly to its neck. I managed to get loose from the net, and as the monster ran by me again I stuck out my pole and tripped it. With a crash, the monster fell down and Verna went flying.

I jumped to my feet and threw the net over the creature. By now Huntley had managed to get down from the tree, and all three of us pounced on the fallen beast as it struggled in the net.

"We did it!" I heard Huntley yell in triumph. "We captured a monster!"

8

Huntley shone the flashlight down on our captive. What we saw in the beam of light was not a monster but a man. A very large, angry man with a beard. Nearby we could see his fishing rod and tackle box. We had ambushed a fisherman! If Huntley's mouth had fallen open any wider he could have swallowed a large pepperoni pizza with extra cheese in one gulp. .

"What's going on here?" the man demanded as he freed himself from the net. "Are you kids crazy or something?"

We had no choice but to tell the truth about the monster. I mean, if we didn't tell him we were trying to ambush a monster it would look like we really *meant* to ambush him.

"You expect me to believe that?" the man snorted. "Monsters? There's no such thing! I fish around here all the time and if there *were* any monsters I'd know about them."

"Would you like some chili?" I asked the man while Huntley and Verna quickly gathered up our gear.

"Now you kids listen to me," the man said, ignor-

39

ing my friendly advances. "There may not be any monsters around here, but a swamp is still a very dangerous place if you aren't careful. So I don't want to catch you anywhere around here again. Understand?"

We beat a hasty retreat, or at least as hasty as we could with me poling the ground in front of us. We didn't speak until we reached the other side of the big pool. There we stopped and looked back at Lost Swamp. It was hard to believe we had dared to enter its eerie depths.

"Well, I guess that ends our exploration of Lost Swamp," I said hopefully. "Right?"

"Wrong!" Huntley replied firmly.

"But the man said—" I began.

"There's something fishy about that guy," Huntley interrupted. "No pun intended."

"What do you mean?" Verna asked.

"There are plenty of good fishing spots around Barkley," Huntley answered. "So what's he doing fishing in a swamp in the dark?"

"Maybe he just doesn't like crowds?" I suggested.

"If there are any fish in Lost Swamp, I bet they're just carp and catfish," Huntley pointed out.

"Then what's he doing in there?" Verna asked.

"The same thing we are," Huntley answered. "Looking for the monster."

"You mean he's a monster hunter like you?" I asked in amazement.

Huntley nodded his head. "He must be. It all fits. Somehow he found out that there is a monster in there and he wants to capture it."

"That rat!" Verna said, clenching her fists. "He wants all the glory for himself."

Huntley agreed. "The last thing he wants is a bunch of kids beating him to the monster. That's why he told us to go away and never come back."

"Then we are coming back?" I asked with a sinking feeling.

"Definitely!" Huntley replied. "All's fair in love and monster hunting."

9

We agreed to go back to the swamp the next day after school. At least, Huntley and Verna agreed and I listened. It seemed as if Monday's classes would never end. For the first time in my life I felt apart from my classmates. Here they were worrying about what the cafeteria was serving for lunch, while I was wondering if I would be alive to see Tuesday morning. I hoped no one would notice how jumpy I was.

At last the final bell rang, and Verna and I headed home to get into our swamp clothes. Afterward we met downtown to wait for Huntley. He takes a bus into Pittsburgh every morning and comes back in the afternoon. Lucky for us the bus stop is right in front of Majersky's Ice Cream Parlor. Verna and I feasted on hot fudge sundaes while we waited.

We had just finished scraping the last precious drops of fudge from our dishes when the bus pulled in. Huntley was carrying his monster-hunting clothes in a shopping bag. He used Majersky's men's room to change.

As he came back out, I could see why some people

think he's a little odd. I mean, here's this chubby little kid walking through a crowded ice cream parlor wearing sunglasses, a knapsack, and a pith helmet. Huntley didn't seem to mind the stares. The man's a real individualist!

"Where's the net?" I asked as we stepped out on the street.

Huntley shook his head. "Today is just a reconnaissance mission. I want to use the daylight to look for more of those webbed footprints."

We had just started up the street when a police car, its lights flashing, screeched to a stop in front of the bank.

"Come on!" Verna cried, breaking into a run.

By the time we reached the front doors, a crowd had gathered. Sam Biffer, the bank's burly security guard, was keeping people back.

"Look," I said, pointing. "There's Mr. Walton. We can ask him what's going on."

Jim Walton is one of the bank's two custodians and a very good friend of ours. He's an older man who has worked there as long as any of us can remember. No matter how busy he is, he always has time to be friendly. He's a real baseball fan and he loves to talk about the Pittsburgh Pirates over ice cream at Majersky's. He always treats.

As Mr. Walton came through the front doors, we

saw that two policemen were walking closely on either side of him. As they passed us, we saw how pale Mr. Walton's wrinkled face was. And then we saw his wrists.

"He's handcuffed!" Verna gasped. "Mr. Walton's handcuffed!"

The policemen put Mr. Walton into a squad car and sped away.

"Let's go around to the side door," Verna said. "We can get in that way."

We went up the alley that ran beside the bank. As we approached the side door, Kevin Kellaway, the bank's other custodian, came out carrying a full plas-

tic garbage bag. Kevin is a young man who once tried out for the Pirates but didn't make the team. We asked him what was going on.

Kevin seemed to be in shock. "I'm not sure. They're saying old Jim was stealing money from the bank."

"That's ridiculous! Mr. Walton isn't a thief," Verna said. "I can't believe it."

Kevin shook his head as he put the garbage next to the other bags lined up in the alley. I thought maybe he was going to cry.

10

We walked in the side door and down the hall toward the bank's office area. To our left, through the glass partitions, we could see the lobby where Huntley's mother and the other tellers were standing in a circle talking.

We found Verna's mother in a conference room at the end of the hall. She was sitting alone at a long table. Her eyes looked sadder than a turkey's at Thanksgiving time.

"Mom?" Verna asked. "Why did the police take Mr. Walton?"

Mrs. Wilkes sighed. "For the past couple of months, money has been disappearing mysteriously from the bank."

"So that's why you've been so upset lately," Verna said. "I thought you were mad at Dad."

Mrs. Wilkes reached out and hugged her daughter. "I'm sorry. I try not to bring work problems home. But it was obvious this was an inside job. It was so upsetting, knowing that one of our own people was stealing."

"Couldn't it have been bookkeeping errors?" Huntley asked.

"I'm afraid not, Huntley," Mrs. Wilkes answered sadly. "We ran countless checks and audits. The only answer was theft."

"But how do you know Mr. Walton is the thief?" I asked.

"We started marking some of the bills, hoping we could trace them. Our security guard found some of them in Jim's locker in the staff lounge. Jim made the mistake of leaving the door ajar so it was easy for Biffer to spot them."

"But Mr. Walton is a custodian," Huntley pointed out. "He doesn't work near the money."

Mrs. Wilkes shrugged her shoulders. "Jim has worked here longer than anyone else. He knows all the ins and outs of the bank's operations. We still don't even know how he got the money out of the building."

"What do you mean, Mrs. Wilkes?" I asked.

"Of course, we called in the authorities. They kept the bank under constant surveillance. Every door, every window was watched twenty-four hours a day. Nothing suspicious happened."

"Couldn't the thief have hidden the money in his clothes or in something he was carrying as he left?" Verna asked.

Mrs. Wilkes shook her head. "Not the amount of money we're missing. We even had a private detective from Pittsburgh working undercover in the bank. She kept a close watch on all the employees from the inside. She saw nothing suspicious."

"Maybe the money never left the bank," Huntley suggested. "Maybe it's still hidden somewhere in the building."

Mrs. Wilkes smiled. "You're a good detective, Huntley. But every nook and cranny has been searched. Nothing."

Just then Mr. Pierce, the bank's senior vice president, stepped into the conference room. He's distinguished looking, with gray hair and a three-piece suit to match. Mr. Pierce always looks like he's just bitten into a sour lemon. He spends a lot of time walking around the bank ordering kids like me to keep our voices down.

Mr. Pierce sat down at the conference table across from Mrs. Wilkes.

"I just talked with police headquarters," he told her. "The detective handling this case said that Jim recently bought his wife an expensive diamond ring at McNary's Jewelry Store. It cost much more than a man with his salary can afford."

"I still can't believe it." Mrs. Wilkes sighed. "Jim was such a good friend to us all."

"Money can bring out the worst in people," Mr. Pierce said in his lemon-like voice. "Even people like Jim."

Mrs. Wilkes looked up as if she suddenly realized we were still in the room. "You kids had better leave, now. And don't say a word to anyone about what you heard here."

We headed back toward the side door. At the end of the hall we could see a man talking with Kevin. After patting Kevin on the shoulder, the man came along the hall toward us. It was Patrick Flynn, the

bank's assistant vice president. Mr. Flynn is as nice as Mr. Pierce is sour. He's a young man with a great sense of humor. Mr. Flynn always wears sharp-looking clothes and he drives a neat black Corvette with a red interior. When he bought it I was the first person he took for a ride. And do you know where he took me? To Three Rivers Stadium to see a Steeler game! Mr. Pierce probably thinks the Steelers are a steel company or something.

Mr. Flynn stopped in front of us. Even though he smiled, his handsome face was lined with worry.

"You kids look the way I used to feel when my great-aunt gave me socks and underwear for my birthday," he said.

"We're worried about Mr. Walton," I told him.

"We all are, Raymond," Mr. Flynn said. "But hang in there. Old Jim's friends here aren't going to give up on him."

With a grim look on his face, Mr. Flynn headed along the hall to the boardroom. Huntley, Verna, and I looked at each other, and I knew we were thinking the same thing. We were Mr. Walton's friends, and we sure weren't going to give up on him either.

Kevin was still standing near the door where Mr. Flynn had left him. Outside, the town's garbage truck had pulled into the alley to make its Monday pickup. Since it blocked the narrow space, we waited beside

Kevin and watched the garbage man as he tossed the plastic bags up into the back of the truck. I didn't know him, but Verna called, "Hi, Charlie," as he swung up after the bags. He stared at her and then waved as the driver started the motor and the truck rumbled away.

Kevin was looking so depressed we just left. We all went straight home. Not even Huntley was in the mood for monster hunting that day.

11

We didn't return to Lost Swamp until Saturday. On Friday, Huntley said he had a new plan. We were to meet at his house early and bring shovels.

Before I left home, my mom gave me a picnic basket full of food. "Take this to Mrs. Walton," she said. "The poor dear must be terribly upset."

Mrs. Wilkes must have had the same idea. Verna came down the sidewalk with a shovel in one hand and a basket of food in the other. And Mrs. English had handed Huntley a goody basket as he walked out his door.

Mr. and Mrs. Walton live in a small white stucco house at the outskirts of town. The yard was alive with spring flowers as we walked up to the door and knocked.

Mrs. Walton is a short, roly-poly woman with sparkling eyes and a big smile. There was no sparkle or smile on her face today. Her eyes were red and puffy from crying.

"Aren't you dears to be thinking of me," she said,

52

giving us each a hug. "Jim and I are certainly blessed with good friends."

As I walked past her I quickly glanced at the diamond ring on her finger. It did look expensive.

We found the kitchen table already loaded with food.

"Kevin was just here and brought all this," Mrs. Walton said. "He even tried to give me money. He's taking this hard. Jim was like a father to him. It was Jim got him the job at the bank."

"We're so sorry about what's happened," Verna said.

Mrs. Walton sniffed. "I just can't believe they suspect Jim. Sure, we're worried about money. What working folks aren't, these days? But Jim would never steal."

"We know he's innocent," Huntley said stoutly.

As we left, I think the three of us were feeling guilty about all the money Mr. Walton had spent buying us ice cream at Majersky's.

This time Huntley wanted to enter the swamp a different way. We followed a dirt road that was well packed down and crisscrossed with huge tire tracks. I had never been this way before.

"By the way," Huntley said in a matter-of-fact voice. "Did you see today's *Bugle*?"

The Barkley *Bugle* is our town's weekly newspa-

lton, bank custodian arrested.

per. It comes out every Saturday morning. News of Mr. Walton's arrest had taken up the entire front page. Both Verna and I nodded our heads.

"And did you see the picture?" Huntley went on. He was talking about a photograph that showed Mr. Walton being taken from the bank by the police.

"So what about it?" Verna demanded.

Huntley reached in his back pocket and handed the picture to us. "Look at the crowd gathered around the front doors."

We looked. I saw it first. A man was standing in the background, watching. A big man with a beard. The fisherman from the swamp!

"What does it mean?" Verna asked.

"Maybe just a coincidence?" I suggested.

"Maybe," Huntley said mysteriously.

After awhile the woods to our right opened up as the road curved around the western rim of Lost Swamp. Seeing it from higher ground made the swamp seem bigger and more mysterious than ever. Looking beyond it, I saw why the road we were on was so well traveled by trucks.

"It's the city dump," I said in surprise.

Verna snorted. "What did you expect to find on the other side of a swamp? Disney World?"

As we got closer we could see people walking around the huge piles of rubbish and dirt. Some of them carried rakes.

"What are those people doing?" I asked.

"Scavenging," Huntley answered. "You never know when someone's going to throw out something valuable."

"Valuables in a garbage dump?" I hooted.

"I heard that Bill Chambers came out here once and

55

found an Adam and the Ants album in perfect condition," Verna pointed out.

I shrugged my shoulders. "I guess it's true what they say. One person's trash is another person's treasure."

Huntley stopped dead in his tracks. "What did you say, Raymond?"

"I said, one person's trash is another person's treasure."

Huntley stood there with this weird smile on his face.

"Earth to Huntley. Earth to Huntley," I said. "Did I say something brilliant?"

But I knew there was no getting through to him when he looked like that. At the moment, J. Huntley English, M.H., was passing the Planet Pluto.

12

No one said much as we entered the swamp. When we did speak, it was in whispers. Lost Swamp is a whispering kind of place. As we moved deeper and deeper into the cool, damp gloom, I found myself looking nervously about. If a horrible swamp monster jumped out and grabbed us, would the people way back at the dump hear our screams? I didn't think so.

To my relief and to Verna and Huntley's obvious disappointment, we encountered no monster. We didn't even find any of the creature's huge webbed footprints. Eventually we came to the island of ground where we had ambushed the fisherman.

"Now what?" Verna asked.

"We dig a hole and cover it up. Sooner or later, the monster will come through and fall into our trap. Then we'll throw the net over him."

"Sounds great!" I said. I liked the idea of the monster in a hole.

"Thank you, Raymond. Now you and Verna dig while I climb the big tree and keep watch."

"Listen, Huntley," Verna hissed. "You're crazier

than I thought if you think we're doing all the digging while you sit around."

"All right," Huntley conceded. "We'll take turns."

That seemed to satisfy Verna, although I noticed as the day wore on that we did most of the digging while Huntley did most of the sitting.

We dug and dug until I was sure we were nearing China. The fact was that by late afternoon Verna and I were only up to our shoulders. Huntley had to come down from the tree to help pull us out.

While Verna and I lay panting on the ground, I heard something scary that made me jump.

"What was that noise?" I asked nervously.

"It's my stomach growling," Verna answered. "Time for this monster hunter to go home for dinner."

"But I don't think it's deep enough," Huntley said, looking critically at our hole.

"Well, it would have been if you had helped," Verna fumed.

"On the other hand, I think it will do," Huntley quickly added.

We gathered thin, brittle tree limbs that had fallen to the ground and laid them across the hole in a web. Then we spread dead leaves and bush branches on top of the limbs. Finally we scattered a thin layer of dirt on top of the whole thing. When we were done, you

58

would never have known that a hole was there.

"Let's call it a day," Huntley said.

"But what if the monster falls in the trap when we're not here to throw the net over it?" I asked. "We'll lose it."

Huntley looked thoughtful. "You're right, Raymond. Maybe we should keep watch here all night."

"Let's call it a day!" I said, jumping to my feet.

We took about three steps and froze. We could hear something coming our way. Verna and Huntley followed me as I dove into a clump of nearby bushes. We just made it. Peering out through the spring leaves, we watched the bearded fisherman step into the clearing. He was still carrying his rod and tackle box. I held my breath, hoping he wouldn't hear my teeth playing "Chopsticks" and catch us. He didn't.

After he disappeared in the direction of the big pool, we left the swamp by way of the city dump.

"It looks like our friend hasn't given up yet," Huntley said grimly.

We were halfway around the swamp when Huntley stopped suddenly and looked down the bank that ran along beside the road.

"What's that?"

Verna and I looked, too, and saw a small pile of trash under the bushes. It was mostly crumpled-up paper towels.

59

"That's funny," Huntley murmured to himself.

"What did you expect to find along the road to the city dump?" Verna snickered. "Orchids?"

"Probably blew off the garbage truck," I suggested.

But Huntley wasn't listening. He just stood there looking first at the trash and then up at the road and then back down again.

By the time we finally started home, I had to admit to myself that Huntley did act a little odd sometimes.

13

First thing after school on Monday, I stopped at the bank to add money to my Christmas Club account.

"Raymond!"

I turned and saw Verna waving to me from the office area.

"What's up?" I asked.

"It's Huntley," Verna answered. "He's playing Sherlock Holmes."

Puzzled, I followed her. Huntley was halfway down the hall, standing on a chair and peering into an air vent in the wall.

"*Now* what do you think you're doing?" Verna demanded.

"Looking for the missing money," Huntley answered as he jumped down.

"My mom said they already searched the bank from top to bottom," Verna pointed out. "It's not here."

"It doesn't hurt to double-check," Huntley replied. "They may have missed a place. We just can't stand around and let an innocent person sit in jail."

"Maybe he did steal the money," Verna said. "The evidence is against him, you know."

"He didn't!" I said angrily. "Mr. Walton wouldn't steal anything!"

"Raymond's right," Huntley said, nodding his head. "Besides, anyone smart enough to fool the authorities wouldn't be dumb enough to leave the money in his locker with the door ajar."

"You're right," Verna said.

"If we find out who framed Mr. Walton, we'll know who the thief is," I said excitedly.

"Maybe it was Mr. Biffer, the security guard," Verna suggested. "He's the one who found the money in Mr. Walton's locker. Or so he says."

"Yeah! Mr. Biffer could have planted the money in the locker and then pretended to find it," I agreed. "Besides, he's a grouch, like Mr. Pierce."

Huntley looked thoughtful. "Being grouchy isn't against the law, Raymond. Still, I think we should check him out as a suspect."

"But first I have to check out the men's room," I said.

"That's about the only place I haven't searched," Huntley said. "Verna? Would you . . . uh . . . check out the ladies' room?"

In the men's room, Huntley climbed up on another

chair to peer into the air vent high on the wall. I was washing my hands when Kevin came in to empty the large metal trash container.

"Kevin," Huntley asked, "how well do you know Mr. Biffer?"

Kevin shook his head. "Not well. Sam Biffer's a strange bird. Keeps to himself."

I crumpled the paper towel I was using into a ball and tossed it into the big garbage bag that Kevin held open for me.

"Two points!" he said, grinning. "You'll make first team yet."

He was referring to the fact that I play second string on the school's basketball team.

"He certainly will," Huntley said, patting me on the back.

I was still blushing with pleasure when we met Verna in the hall.

"Your face looks like tomato soup," Verna told me. "Nothing in the ladies' room," she said to Huntley.

"Let's go around and talk to the other people who work here," I suggested. "That's what real detectives do."

Huntley shook his head. "I tried that. My mom told me to stop bothering people."

"Did you find out anything?" Verna asked.

"Mom did say that the money came up missing only on Mondays. She also said no money has disappeared since Mr. Walton was arrested."

"What are we going to do?" I cried helplessly.

"Tomorrow after school one of us will tail Mr. Biffer. The other two will go to the swamp and check the trap."

I groaned. Some choice!

14

I chose Mr. Biffer, even though I was a little afraid of him. The bank's security guard is a big man with a huge beer belly that hangs out over his gun belt. He walks around the bank and stares at everyone with hard, beady little eyes. But, as scared as I was of him, he was still better than Lost Swamp with its elusive monster.

After school I stopped at Majersky's for an ice cream soda to give me strength. Then I bought a newspaper and sat down on a bench across from the bank. An hour later the bank employees began leaving. I hid behind the paper so that Huntley's and Verna's mothers wouldn't see me.

I watched Mr. Flynn, the assistant vice president, come out and get into his Corvette and drive away.

Next, Mr. Pierce, the senior vice president, came out with Mr. Biffer. They stood in front of the bank and talked for awhile. Then Mr. Pierce walked away down the street. Mr. Biffer locked the bank doors and turned in the opposite direction.

I rolled up my paper and quickly crossed the street, keeping a safe distance behind Mr. Biffer. I tried not to act suspicious. Every once in awhile my quarry would stop to look in a store window. Whenever he did, I tried to do the same. Unfortunately, I never seemed to be in front of a window. If Mr. Biffer had looked back he would have seen this strange kid standing on the sidewalk carefully studying the brick walls of the buildings. Lucky for me, he didn't turn around.

Near the corner of Main and Chestnut, the big security guard went into Jay's Donut Shop. I peeked in the window. Even though there was only one man sitting at the long counter, Mr. Biffer went and sat right next to him. Quickly, I went in and slipped into a booth.

When the waitress came I ordered my usual—two jelly donuts and a mug of hot chocolate with extra marshmallows. While I ate, I watched Mr. Biffer and the other man. They talked softly without looking at each other. I could tell they didn't want anyone to know they were together. I wished I could hear what they were saying but I didn't dare go near them. Mr. Biffer might recognize me and get suspicious.

After a few minutes, Mr. Biffer got up and left the shop. I wanted to follow him, but I also wanted to see who he'd been talking to so secretively. I didn't have to wait long. In a few moments, the other man slid off his stool and headed for the door. When I got a look at him, I was so surprised I almost spit raspberry jelly all over the booth. It was the fisherman from the swamp!

I quickly decided to follow him. I could follow the security guard anytime. I left money for my snack on the table and hurried outside. I hit the street in time to see the fisherman get into his car and drive away. I looked around for Mr. Biffer but he was gone.

I had lost both of them. But I didn't care. I had found out something important and I couldn't wait to tell Huntley and Verna.

15

Huntley and Verna were amazed when I reported what I had seen. Their own mission had been a bust. Our trap still hadn't been sprung, and there was no sign of the monster.

"Mr. Biffer is now our prime suspect," Huntley declared as we sat in his office at home.

"How did he do it?" Verna asked.

Huntley looked thoughtful. "The way I see it is this. Somehow during the day he would get his hands on the money. Then he'd hide it someplace in the bank. Someplace where no one would find it."

"And then?"

"And then later he'd sneak the money out of the building."

"But how?" I asked. "Mrs. Wilkes said the bank was closely watched inside and out."

"But I bet it wasn't watched as closely on weekends when the bank is closed and no one is there," Huntley pointed out.

"Yeah!" I said excitedly. "And, being the security guard, Mr. Biffer has keys to all the bank's doors."

"So it would be easy for him to slip in there over the weekend and get the money out of his hiding place," Huntley concluded. "No one would suspect the security guard."

"And if someone did catch him in the bank on the weekend," I pointed out, "he could just say he was checking the place out. After all, that's his job."

"A good alibi," Huntley agreed. "And with the bank vault locked until Monday, no one would suspect him of anything."

Verna was clenching her fists and looking very mean. "When he had stolen as much money as he dared, he needed someone to take the blame. He stashed some of the marked bills in poor Mr. Walton's locker and then pretended to find them."

"O.K.," I said. "That much I understand. But where does the phony fisherman fit in?"

Huntley shook his head. "I don't know yet. We know from the newspaper photo that he was at the bank the day Mr. Walton was arrested."

"And we know he knows Mr. Biffer," I added. "And that they meet on the sly."

"I guess you were wrong about his being a monster hunter like you," Verna said to Huntley.

"But if he isn't a monster hunter, and he's not a fisherman, then what's he doing at the swamp?" I asked.

Huntley was silent for a minute. "Lost Swamp has secrets," he finally said in a mysterious voice. "It's time we found out what they are."

"Yeah," Verna agreed. "Before time runs out on Mr. Walton."

16

"I've got bad news," Verna said as she caught up with me on my way to school the next morning.

"Figures," I muttered grumpily.

It looked as if it was going to be one of those days. First, my little brother had buried my wristwatch in his oatmeal at breakfast. Then, as I cut across our neighbors' yard, I'd stepped in a little present left there by their dog. We were having a history test first period and I hadn't studied for it. And now Verna comes running up with bad news.

"Mom told me the bank *was* watched on weekends," Verna went on, "and no one was seen going in or out."

"Great!" I said as I angrily kicked a poor innocent stone. "If we can't figure out how that guard stole the money, we'll never be able to prove Mr. Walton is innocent."

My day continued downhill after that. The history test was a disaster. The cafeteria served tuna casserole for lunch. And during last period, Verna kept throwing spitballs at the back of my head, making the whole class snicker.

After school I fled to Huntley's house. I knew if anyone could cheer me up he could. Nothing seems to discourage or depress J. Huntley English.

But when I got there, his mother said he had come home from school and gone for a walk in the country. I knew what that meant. Huntley had gone alone to Lost Swamp.

I sure didn't relish the idea of wandering around the swamp looking for him. But Huntley's my friend and I felt I should be with him in case he got into trouble. Besides, I was curious about what he was up to.

I had just left the town limits when I heard the loud roar of a truck coming up behind me. As I stepped farther off the side of the road, the town's garbage truck stopped beside me.

"Hey, Raymond," a voice called out from the truck's cab. "What are you doing way out here?"

I looked through the open window and saw Geoffrey Powell's father sitting behind the wheel.

"I'm on my way to Lost Swamp," I answered.

"Heck of a place to go," Mr. Powell said with a grin. "Hop in and I'll give you a lift. We go right by it on our way to the dump."

I glanced enviously at the back of the dump truck.

Mr. Powell laughed. "Go ahead and ride on top if you want. The view is better if you can stand the smell, *and* Prince Charles's swelled head."

I wondered what he was talking about as I climbed up in back. Prince Charles turned out to be the same man I had seen picking up the bank's garbage the other day. He was wearing a cutoff tee shirt that showed off his bulging muscles and tattoos.

"You must be Prince Charles," I said as I stepped over the garbage bags to where he was standing. "I'm Raymond."

"Don't call me that," he growled. "My name is Charlie."

I turned red. "I'm sorry. Mr. Powell called you Prince Charles. I thought it was your nickname or something."

"Powell's just jealous because I'm getting out of this. I told him I'm not spending the rest of *my* life picking up other people's garbage like he is," Charlie said as he lit a cigarette.

The truck rumbled up the highway for awhile and then slowed to turn off on the road to the dump.

"Better hang onto the side," Charlie advised me. "When we hit the dirt road this old buggy does some mean shaking."

He was right. As we bounced along I felt like a

73

marble rattling around in a boxcar. At one point I lost my grip and fell into a pile of garbage bags. Charlie howled with laughter.

Up ahead I could see Lost Swamp stretched out to our right. And there, sitting on a fallen log beside the road, was Huntley. He was staring down at the swamp through a pair of binoculars.

I called out to Mr. Powell to stop the truck. Huntley looked up in amazement as I jumped down. Mr. Powell beeped the horn and the truck rumbled away toward the dump. Charlie waved from up on top so I guess he wasn't really mad at me for calling him Prince Charles.

I sat down on the log and told Huntley about Verna's bad news. It didn't faze him a bit. He just sat there grinning like a cat at a fish fry.

"What are you smiling about?" I finally demanded.

"I'm smiling because of you, Raymond," he answered. "You're a real inspiration."

"I am?" I asked in amazement.

"Come on!" he said. "Let's go to my office."

As I followed him back to town, I felt a hundred percent better and I didn't know why.

17

"This is one *weird* room," Verna muttered.

She had been acting grumpy ever since she walked into Huntley's office and gotten tangled up in his dinosaur mobile.

"Thank you," the Monster Hunter replied proudly.

"So what's our next move?"

"A big stakeout this Friday night," Huntley answered.

"Keep going," Verna prodded.

"We'll divide up," Huntley went on. "Verna, you'll watch our trap in the swamp. Raymond, you'll watch the big pool where the creature came out of the water."

"And what will you be doing while we slosh around that soggy swamp?" Verna demanded. "Sitting in here talking to Dracula's head?"

"No," Huntley answered coolly. "I'll be tailing Mr. Biffer."

"Maybe I'd better do that," I suggested hopefully.

"No," Huntley answered. "You already did once. He might get suspicious if you do again. And he knows

Verna too well because she's the boss' daughter. That leaves me."

"So where do you think all this is leading us?" Verna asked.

Huntley sat back in his chair, looking very thoughtful. "I'm not sure yet. All I have in my mind are pieces of the puzzle. They haven't formed a picture yet."

"That does it!" Verna said, rolling her eyes upward. "I've had enough of this mumbo jumbo. I'm leaving."

"I sure hope you don't think I'm going to Lost Swamp alone on Friday night," I said, after Verna had stomped out of the room.

"Don't worry," Huntley reassured me. "Verna will be there. She won't want to miss out on the action."

"Did you say action?" I gulped.

Huntley nodded grimly but said no more. I looked down and saw that I was patting Dracula's head with a sweaty palm.

18

Huntley was correct about Verna. She was right there
with me that windy Friday night as we headed out on
our mission. I was glad for her company, especially
when we entered the gloomy chill of Lost Swamp.

"You hide in the bushes and watch the pool," she
whispered. "I'll climb the tree near the trap and keep
a lookout from there."

I nodded glumly as she disappeared deeper into the
swamp, carrying the net and rope over her shoulder.
It was just about dark as I settled in the bushes to wait.

I didn't have to wait long. Almost immediately
something came crashing my way. My heart felt like
a basketball at a Boston Celtic's game.

Although there was a moon, the wind was driving
rolling clouds across it. When the creature finally
shuffled awkwardly by my hiding place, I could only
see its outline.

I watched in fascination as it slipped into the pool
and disappeared. A few seconds later, the water lit up
in an eerie green glow. I wanted to run and get Verna
but I didn't. It was a good thing, because in another
minute the beast came out of the water onto the bank.

This time I forgot to be scared because I finally got a good look at it. My mouth fell open in surprise. It wasn't a monster at all. It was a scuba diver!

The diver was wearing a dark green wetsuit with a small dark green tank strapped to his back. Algae and scum from the surface of the pool covered his head and shoulders. In one hand, he was carrying a dripping plastic garbage bag. In the other was an underwater flashlight. The diver switched off the light before removing the mask, so I couldn't see who it was.

It was easy following the diver into the swamp because the flippers made walking on land awkward. Now I knew where the webbed footprint we had found in the mud came from.

The diver finally stopped in our clearing where the ground was firmer. I ducked into some bushes when he put down the garbage bag. I watched as he turned the flashlight back on and pulled a knife from his belt. Slashing open the plastic bag, he began dumping its contents on the ground.

At first nothing came out but piles and piles of crumpled-up paper towels. I couldn't figure out what was happening. And then something fell out that wasn't trash. It was money!

Not until the man turned to stuff the money in a cloth sack did I get a good look at his face. Talk about shocks. It was Kevin!

19

I saw red. I mean, I was mad. Mr. Walton had been like a father to Kevin. And now he was in jail, taking the blame for what Kevin had done. Kevin was the real thief!

As you've probably already noticed, I'm not the bravest person in the world. But I was so mad at Kevin that I wanted to march right out and confront him then. Someone beat me to it. A flashlight was suddenly turned on to my right and a man stepped into the clearing. I quickly ducked back down in the bushes.

Kevin stood in the beam of light with his hands raised. He was still dripping pool water and I could tell he was real scared. When I saw who the newcomer was, my mouth fell open. It was Charlie, the sanitation worker I rode in the garbage truck with. And then I saw why Kevin had his hands up. Charlie was pointing a nasty-looking gun at him.

"Helping yourself to *our* money, Kevin?" Charlie growled.

Kevin shook his head. "I wasn't taking it for myself, Charlie. I was going to return it to the bank."

79

"Now why would you do a stupid thing like that?" Charlie sneered.

"No one ever said anything about pinning the heists on old Jim," Kevin said angrily. "Maybe, if I take the money back to the bank, they'll let him go."

"So you want *us* to go to jail instead?" Charlie asked.

"No." Kevin shook his head. "I'll leave the money with a note saying that Jim's innocent."

Charlie gave a harsh laugh. "You're not leaving anything anywhere but here. I'm afraid Lost Swamp is about to claim another victim."

I had to do something. But what? And then I remembered that Verna was in the tree above Kevin and Charlie. As I looked up into the dark branches the moon peeked out from the clouds. In the fleeting silver second I saw Verna scampering from limb to limb. She was about to do something and, knowing Verna Wilkes, I knew it would be something daring.

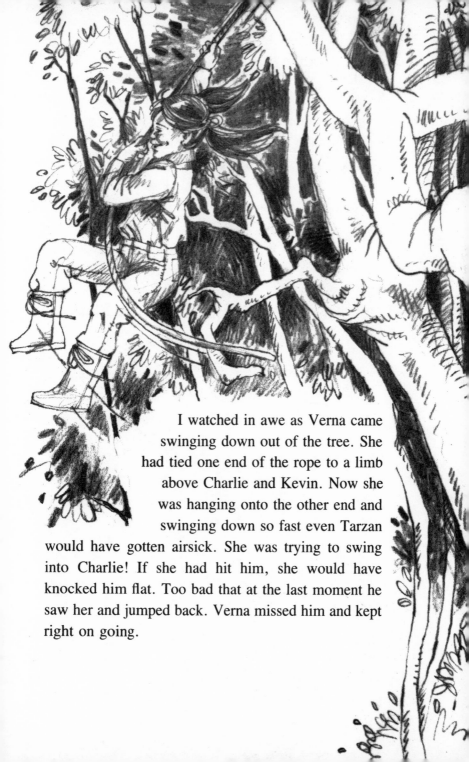

I watched in awe as Verna came swinging down out of the tree. She had tied one end of the rope to a limb above Charlie and Kevin. Now she was hanging onto the other end and swinging down so fast even Tarzan would have gotten airsick. She was trying to swing into Charlie! If she had hit him, she would have knocked him flat. Too bad that at the last moment he saw her and jumped back. Verna missed him and kept right on going.

Charlie and Kevin watched in amazement as Verna swung up, stopped in midair, and helplessly began swinging down. Back and forth she went like a pendulum, going slower and slower until she was suspended straight down from the limb.

"Just thought I'd drop in," she said, letting go of the rope and leaping nimbly to the ground. "I'm a real swinger, you know."

That Verna! I knew she must be scared silly but she wasn't about to let anyone know. Not even someone who was pointing a gun at her.

Now that Verna was a prisoner, there was only one person left to save the day. Me!

20

I decided the best thing to do was to run and get help. I wished I could do something more daring but I couldn't risk getting caught like Verna. I was the last hope.

At first I had to go slow because I didn't want them to hear me crashing through the underbrush. Not until I reached the big pool did I dare break into a run. I was trying so hard to make up time that I almost didn't see the figure coming toward me around the pool. I dove headfirst into some bushes and watched as the man came closer.

Not until he was almost on top of me did I see who it was. My heart leaped for joy. It was my friend Mr. Flynn, the bank's assistant vice president. He was wearing jeans and a black sweatshirt. I almost hadn't recognized him dressed like that.

"Mr. Flynn!" I shouted, jumping out of the bushes.

Mr. Flynn nearly jumped out of his jeans and sweatshirt.

"Raymond Almond!" he exclaimed. "What are you doing here at this hour?"

I breathlessly explained the situation in the swamp.

"So you see," I finished in a rush, "I'm going to get the police."

"No need," he said, putting his hand on my shoulder. "I've been investigating this case on my own. That's why I'm here now. I'll go into the swamp with you and we'll check this thing out."

I shook my head. "I really think I'd better get the police. Charlie has a gun."

The grip on my shoulder tightened. Tightened hard. It didn't feel like the grip of a friend. I tried to break away, but Mr. Flynn put a hammerlock around my head and dragged me back into the swamp. When we got to the clearing, he pushed me over next to Verna and Kevin.

Charlie waved his gun in our direction. "I was right about our *buddy* here," he snarled. "Would you believe he was going to give the money back to the bank?"

Mr. Flynn nodded his head grimly. "You always did have a conscience, Kevin. Too bad."

"What are we going to do with these snoopy kids?" Charlie asked.

"You're going to let them go," a voice from the bushes answered.

Everyone spun around in surprise. I couldn't believe what I saw. Into the clearing, as coolly as you please, strolled Huntley. He was dressed in his full monster-hunting getup, and he walked toward us with all the dignity of a king in his court.

Charlie lunged at Huntley. "Why, you little! . . ."

Suddenly Mr. Biffer, the bank guard, and the mysterious fisherman came running out of the darkness. The fisherman knocked the gun out of Charlie's hand while Mr. Biffer tackled him. As Charlie went down with a thud, Mr. Flynn bolted.

"He's getting away!" I hollered.

While Mr. Biffer sat on Charlie, the fisherman took off after Mr. Flynn. As things turned out, he needn't have hurried. The assistant vice president only got about twenty feet away before he disappeared. It was as if the earth had swallowed him up.

And then I realized it had. He had fallen into our monster trap!

The fisherman quickly fished him out and put on the handcuffs. Then he came over and angrily looked down at Huntley.

"I thought I told you to stay behind. You could have been killed."

Huntley just stood there looking up at him. "A monster hunter never flinches in the face of danger."

The fisherman couldn't help smiling.

"Who is this guy, anyway?" I asked.

Huntley grinned. "Raymond. Verna. I'd like you to meet Sergeant Michael Tucker of the Pennsylvania State Police."

21

Everything finally got sorted out the next morning when Verna's mother had us to the house for breakfast. Sergeant Tucker was there, along with Mr. Biffer, Huntley, myself, and, of course, Verna. Mr. and Mrs. Walton were the guests of honor. Sergeant Tucker had arranged to get Mr. Walton immediately released from jail.

"So tell me, Sergeant," Mrs. Wilkes said as she passed him the scrambled eggs. "Just how did our assistant vice president manage to fool us for so long?"

Sergeant Tucker winked at Huntley. "Why don't you tell her?"

Huntley grinned. "On Mondays, Mr. Flynn would slip money into his pockets and go to the men's room. He then put the money into the trash container, making sure it was buried under paper towels before he left. As you know, one of Kevin's jobs is to empty all the bank's wastepaper baskets. Kevin would go into the men's room and dump the stuff from the basket, money and all, into a garbage bag. Then he'd tie the bag closed with a double knot and put it out in the alley with the other garbage bags.

"Monday is the day Mr. Powell and Charlie pick up the bank's trash. Charlie would throw the garbage bags onto the truck, keeping an eye out for the one with the double knot. As the truck passed Lost Swamp on its way to the dump, Charlie would throw the double-knotted garbage bag over the side into the bushes. That's why he always rode on top. Mr. Powell was too busy driving to notice what was going on in the back."

"Yeah," I said snapping my fingers, "and one time a bag must have broken open when it hit the ground. We saw the paper towels in the bushes."

"Later," Huntley continued, "Charlie would go back and carry the bag into the swamp. First he would put a heavy rock in the bag and then make sure the bag was watertight. Then he threw the bag into the pool so it would sink to the bottom next to the others he had thrown in earlier. It was the perfect hiding place."

"So who was the scuba diver we saw in the background of our movie?" Verna asked.

Sergeant Tucker laughed. "Charlie was your swamp monster. Flynn had him put on his scuba gear and dive to the bottom of the pool to check on the bags. Flynn wanted to make sure the bags weren't breaking open

"But the clincher was seeing you jump down from that garbage truck near the spot where we found the paper towels in the bushes. I noticed then how Charlie was riding up on top instead of in the cab."

"Gee!" I smiled. "I guess I was a big help."

Verna meanwhile had been standing there looking like a dog in front of an empty food dish.

"What's the matter with you?" I asked.

Verna shrugged her shoulders. "I'm really glad we were able to help Mr. Walton. But I did have my heart set on capturing a real live monster."

"Don't worry," Huntley said in his most solemn voice. "There are monsters, and we'll catch one yet."

23

In all the excitement I had forgotten E-Day. Embarrassment Day. The day the projects were due and the whole class would see me making a fool of myself.

"Class," Mrs. Phillips said first thing in the morning. "Since Verna's film played such an important part in solving a serious crime, I've suggested to the principal that we show it to the entire school."

I groaned. I might have known this would happen. In a small town like Barkley, news travels fast. By now everyone had heard about our part in capturing the bank robbers.

Before lunch, the whole school gathered in the auditorium and watched the film. Soon everyone was laughing hysterically. And then something unexpected happened. I started laughing, too. And why not? Comedians like Steve Martin and Robin Williams work hard at making people laugh. When people laugh they forget their problems. And here I was, making a lot of people happy.

During lunch everyone came up and congratulated me. I realized that they had been laughing with me and not at me. I felt good until I got back to class. Then I felt a letdown. The mystery of the horrible swamp monster was solved. All the excitement was over. What now?

And then I remembered Huntley's words: "There are monsters, and we'll catch one yet." And you know something? I believe him!

Drew, Liz, and Quincy

About the Author:

Drew Stevenson was born on Christmas Day, 1947, in Washington, Pennsylvania. He was graduated from Bethany College in West Virginia with a B.A. in English, and received his Master's Degree in Library Science from the University of Pittsburgh.

Since 1971, he has worked at the Tompkins County Public Library in Ithaca, New York, first as assistant children's librarian and currently as Adult Services librarian. He hosts a library television show called ''What's Happening?'' on the local cable channel.

The author and his wife, Liz, share their home with Quincy, a very remarkable cat. Drew Stevenson's first book was *The Ballad of Penelope Lou . . . and Me* (Crossing Press) with illustrations by Marcia Sewell. He writes the mystery and suspense book review column for *School Library Journal* and—''I love mystery stories!'' he says.

About the Artist:

Susan Swan was born in Coral Gables, Florida, and received her Master of Fine Arts degree from Florida State University. She has illustrated many text and trade books for children. She lives in Westport, Connecticut, with her collection of windup toys.